A Place Where Hurricanes Happen

For Mia Kristin Smith and the children and staff of the 2006 Gretna Community Arts Camp,
and for children everywhere who have survived their own personal storms —R.W.

For New Orleans — S.S.

Text copyright © 2010 by Renée Watson
Cover art and interior illustrations copyright © 2010 by Shadra Strickland

Published in the United States by Dragonfly Books, an imprint of Random House Children's Books, a division of Random House LLC,
a Penguin Random House Company, New York.
Originally published in hardcover in the United States by Random House Children's Books, New York, in 2010.

Dragonfly Books with the colophon is a registered trademark of Random House LLC.

Visit us on the Web! randomhouse.com/kids

Educators and librarians, for a variety of teaching tools, visit us at RHTeachersLibrarians.com

The Library of Congress has cataloged the hardcover edition of this work as follows:
Watson, Renée.
A place where hurricanes happen / by Renée Watson ; illustrated by Shadra Strickland. — 1st ed.
p. cm.
Summary: Told in alternating voices, four friends from the same New Orleans neighborhood describe what happens to them and their community when they
are separated, then reunited, as a result of Hurricane Katrina.
ISBN 978-0-375-85609-9 (trade) — ISBN 978-0-375-95609-6 (lib. bdg.)
1. Hurricane Katrina, 2005—Juvenile fiction. [1. Hurricane Katrina, 2005—Fiction. 2. Neighborhood—Fiction.
3. Community life—Louisiana—New Orleans—Fiction. 4. New Orleans (La.)—Fiction.] I. Strickland, Shadra, ill. II. Title.
PZ7.W32868Pl 2010 [E]—dc22 2009017826

ISBN 978-0-385-37668-6 (pbk.)

MANUFACTURED IN CHINA
10 9 8 7 6 5 4 3 2 1
First Dragonfly Books Edition

A Place Where Hurricanes Happen

by Renée Watson • illustrated by Shadra Strickland

DRAGONFLY BOOKS ———🪰—— NEW YORK

We're from New Orleans,
a place where hurricanes happen.
But that's only the bad side.

Adrienne

Playing outside is my favorite thing to do.
I play with my friends
Keesha, Michael and Tommy,
who live down the block.
Our favorite game is hide-and-go-seek.
No one can ever find me.
I hide in the best places.
Keesha is easy to find.
She hides behind the same tree every time—
the one in front of Michael's house.
Always giggling to herself
'cause she thinks she's tricked us.

We play together all day.
Me, Keesha, Michael and Tommy.
Until we are called to come inside.
Eat dinner. Take a bath.
And I can't wait till tomorrow,
when I can come outside and play again.

Michael

Jasmine is my little sister.
She is six. I am eight.
I get to do more things than her
because I am the oldest.
I am the one who makes sure Jasmine doesn't get hurt
when we go outside to play.

I am the one who can walk down the block all by myself.
I am the one who picks Jasmine up from her babysitter's house.
As I walk down the street, I see my neighbors on their porches.
My ears are full of gospel, hip-hop and jazz
blasting from car stereos.
Everybody says hello on my block
and I say hello back, even if I don't know their names.

When I get to Mrs. Johnson's house,
she has a cold glass of sweet tea waiting for me.
We sit on Mrs. Johnson's porch, drinking our tea
and adding to the puzzle she's working on.
When it's time to go, I take Jasmine's hand
and hold it the whole way home
because that is what big brothers do.

Keesha

Momma's cooking dinner,
making my favorite foods:
jambalaya with corn bread.
And I get to help.
I sprinkle spices in the pot
and they dance and twirl
in Momma's thick sauce
as she stirs all the ingredients
with her wooden spoon.
Momma says soon it'll be time to eat.
And I can't wait 'cause I know
it's going to taste so good.

Tommy

I do not like sharin' a room with my older brother.
His clothes take up all the space in the closet.
He gets three of the dresser drawers
and I only get one.
His posters cover most of the wall.
And he gets the bottom bunk.
But worst of all, he snores.
Tonight I was dreamin' about havin' my own room.
But now I'm wide awake.

Keesha

I have sixteen teddy bears.
My momma's been collecting them
since the day I was born.
My black bear is the biggest of them all.
His marble eyes watch over me at night.
My pink teddy bear listens to all of my secrets.
And I always choose one to sleep with.
My older brother and sister say I'm too old
to sleep with
teddy bears.
But my momma
says it's okay and she
buys me another one.
Now I have seventeen.

Michael

I love sitting under the tree in front of my house.
Sometimes I sit under this tree all by myself
and I draw pictures.
Today, I sit under my tree
and I draw my neighbors.
Adrienne asks me if I want to play at her house.
I'll go over later.
Right now I am drawing pictures
and sitting under my favorite tree.
It's giving me all the shade I need to keep cool.

Adrienne

The calm before the storm
is what my granny calls it.
The sky don't look gray at all.
Seems like the sun is gonna shine forever.
Granny says that even though it don't look like it,
a storm's on the way.
So Keesha has to go home.
But soon, the storm will be over
and we'll be outside playing again.
The sky don't look gray at all.
Seems like the sun is gonna shine forever.

Tommy

My daddy's boardin' up the house
'cause the man on the news said a storm is comin'.
Don't know why he wants to save this house.
It's raggedy.
Sometimes when it rains,
the water comes through the roof.
Hits me on my head. Makes puddles on the floor.
I watch my momma pack.
We're leavin' tonight. Goin' to my aunt's house.
Momma tells me I can bring
two of my favorite things.
I can't wait to leave New Orleans.
Road trip with my family.
Houston is just five hours away.

Adrienne

Granny says they named the storm Katrina.
Hurricane Katrina.
She's coming to New Orleans
with her big wind and heavy rain.
Even though my granny said we weren't leaving,
we packed up our stuff today.
We're going to Baton Rouge.
Gonna stay with my granny's friend.

Michael

Tommy's family packed up and left.
And Adrienne is leaving too.
I give her the picture I drew yesterday.
Guess we're not playing together tomorrow.

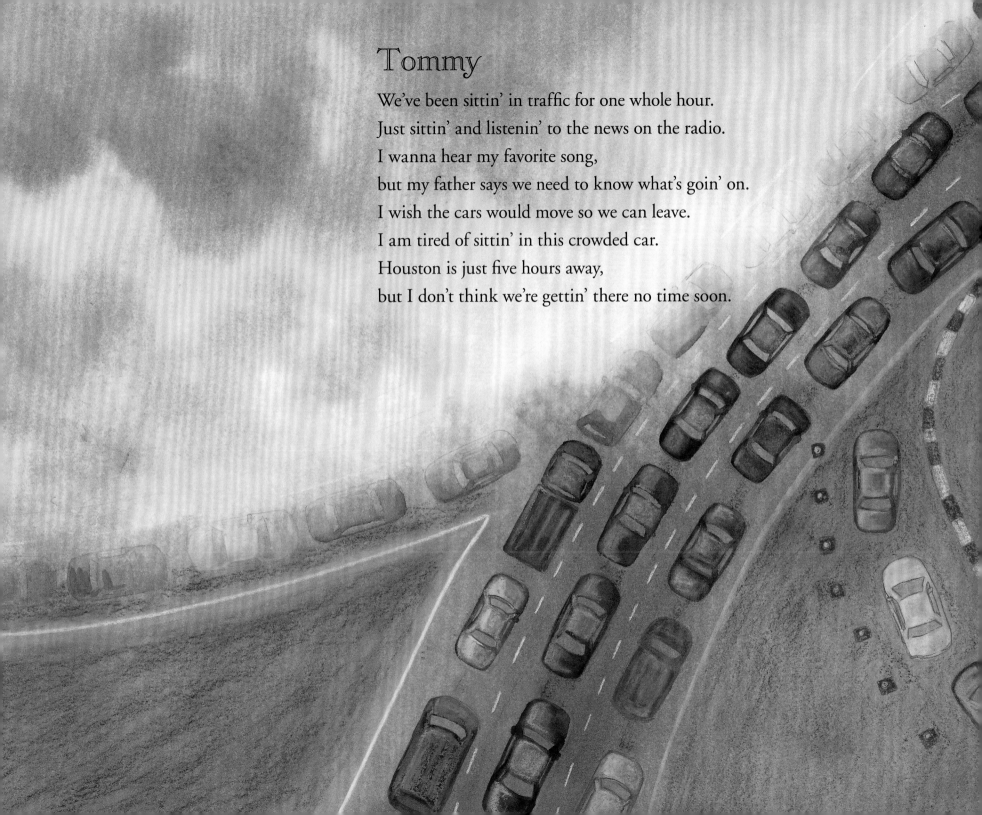

Tommy

We've been sittin' in traffic for one whole hour.

Just sittin' and listenin' to the news on the radio.

I wanna hear my favorite song,

but my father says we need to know what's goin' on.

I wish the cars would move so we can leave.

I am tired of sittin' in this crowded car.

Houston is just five hours away,

but I don't think we're gettin' there no time soon.

Michael

Cars are turned upside down
and the street sign is floating in the water.
Daddy tells us to get to the attic
as fast as we can.
I take Jasmine's hand and I hold it tight,
like big brothers do.
She's too scared to look out the window,
but I'm not.

I look out the window
and I see the whole block swimming in water.
Furniture, clothes and toys are swirling in the flood.
Roofs are crumbling and windows are shattering.
Big winds have come and trees are breaking.
And all I can see is more water rising.
So I look away and I squeeze Jasmine's hand
real tight because now I am scared too.

Keesha

I'm waiting in line at the Superdome
for the buses to come to take us to a safe place.
My family has been waiting for five days.
Finally, the buses are here. The line is long.
I can't see where it begins or ends.
I'm thirsty, but there's no water to drink.
The woman next to my family lives in the same parish,
but we've never met before.
She shares her water with me.
I open the bottle and drink as fast as I can,
but Momma tells me to slow down, save some for later.
I thank the woman.
I think maybe I'll send her one of my teddy bears
when we get back home.

Michael

A rescue team came and saved my family.
They took us to a shelter.
Today, we're home for the first time in six months.
We're moving into a trailer.
Things aren't what they used to be.
The houses on our block are damaged bad.
Things aren't what they used to be.
My tree is the only tree on the block still standing.
Things aren't what they used to be.
Katrina turned New Orleans inside out.
She crumbled roofs, blew away houses
and put everything that was *inside* out on the street.
Things aren't what they used to be.

Katrina took away my drawings,
my markers and my paper.
She even took some of my neighbors away.
There are numbers and words written on
Mrs. Johnson's house.
I ask my mother what they mean.
She tells me Mrs. Johnson isn't coming back.
She's gone forever.
Things aren't what they used to be.
I miss the people who are gone.
Even the neighbors whose names I never knew.

Tommy

My father says not to complain.
He says not to pout when I don't get my way.
He tells me to stop thinkin' 'bout what I don't have.
He says I have more than others
and to be thankful for that.
But it's hard to be thankful.
Livin' in Houston isn't fun at all.
I am sleepin' on the floor
'cause the house is so crowded.
And I have to share everything.
I don't understand why my dad says
some got it worse.
But then he turns on the TV
and we watch the news.
I think of Adrienne, Michael and Keesha
and I hope they are not the ones
my dad is talkin' 'bout.

Keesha

Dear Adrienne,

We're staying in a trailer outside our broken house.

Katrina took my teddy bears away. I don't have any.

I play outside with Michael, but it's not the same

without you and Tommy.

Adrienne, don't forget about me, hear?

I'm still your best friend.

The only friend that can twirl the rope at

the perfect speed so you don't trip.

Don't forget how I keep the night-light on for you

when you spend the night.

Don't forget how good I can dance

and how I show you how to move too.

We can still be best friends, right?

Even though we're not living on the same block.

Adrienne, don't forget about me, hear?

Don't forget I'm still your best friend.

       Love,

       Keesha

Adrienne

Dear Keesha,

Granny told me the best news today.

Our house is fixed and we're coming back home.

Keesha, I didn't forget any of you.

I remember how Tommy likes baseball

and how Michael loves to draw.

And I didn't forget how much you like teddy bears.

> Love,
>
> Adrienne

Tommy

We're goin' back to New Orleans.
Got family and friends to see.
We're goin' to the French Quarter,
eat a snowball and some beignets.
We're goin' to listen to the street bands
playin' on the corner.
We're goin' back home.
No traffic jam today.
We'll be there in no time.

Michael

Adrienne and her granny are back.
They brought gifts for all of us.
They give Keesha a white teddy bear
and Tommy a baseball.
But I get the best gift of all—
a sketchbook and markers.
Adrienne hands me the picture I drew
of the people on our block.
It is in a frame.
Our block is different now.
Most of these people haven't come back.
My mother says some live in other states,
and some are in Heaven now.

Me, Adrienne, Tommy and Keesha
want to do something special for our neighbors,
so Adrienne and Keesha make a wreath of flowers
and we hang the picture and the flowers on my tree.
That way, if any of our neighbors ever come back
or if they can see us from Heaven,
they will know that we didn't forget about them.

Adrienne

A whole year has gone by
and a lot of things are different,
but some things are the same.
I've still got friends.
And today, I get to play.
It's sunny outside and me, Keesha,
Michael and Tommy are
playing hide-and-go-seek.
Granny says Katrina's the worst storm
that's come this way in a long time.
She says it'll take a while
for things to get back to how they used to be.
But today, we don't have to worry about that.
Today, no one has to go home early.
Today, we'll sit on Granny's porch
and eat po'boy sandwiches.
Today, we'll play till the sun goes down.
Today, the sky don't look gray at all.
Seems like the sun is gonna shine forever.

We're from New Orleans.
We're from a place where people are tough.
Tough because of the things they've been through,
the things they've seen.
We're from New Orleans,
a place where hurricanes happen.
But that's only the bad side.